To Jackson & Mary Matthes —

Best Wishes!

Robert Lull

11/20/08

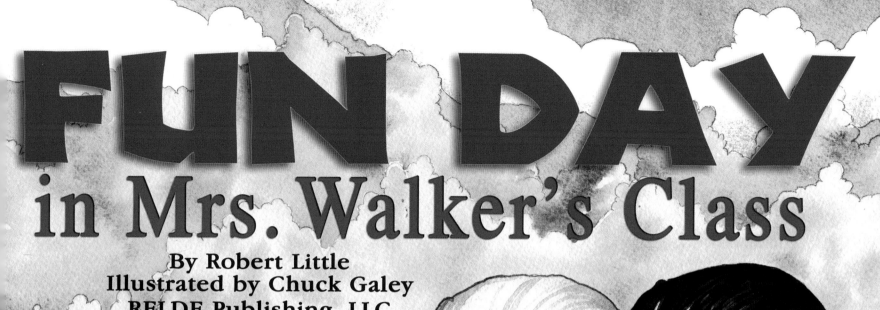

FUN DAY
in Mrs. Walker's Class

By Robert Little
Illustrated by Chuck Galey
RELDE Publishing, LLC

RELDE
PUBLISHING, LLC

Publisher's Cataloging-In-Publication Data

Little, Robert, 1959-
    FUN DAY in Mrs. Walker's Class / by Robert Little ; illustrated by Chuck Galey.
        p. : ill. ; cm.
      ISBN-10: 0-9701863-6-3
      ISBN-13: 978-0-9701863-6-2

1. Social skills in children--Study and teaching--Juvenile fiction. 2.
Ability in children--Juvenille fiction. 3. School contests--Juvenile
fiction. 4. Games--Fiction. I. Galey, Chuck. II. Title.

PS3562.I88 F86 2005
813.6   2005906287

For additional books and to contact Robert Little for speaking
engagements:

RELDE Publishing, LLC
P.O. Box 21304, Jackson, MS 39289
www.reldepublishing.com
www.robertlittlespeaker.com
1-800-489-3439

DEDICATIONS

For all teachers—for all that you do. Thank you.
—R.L.

To Mrs. McDaniel's Class. Thanks for all your help.
—C.G.

The day before FUN DAY, Mrs. Walker was trying to think of things for her third grade class to do. FUN DAY is a day set aside in May of each year for students to play games, have parties, go on field trips or do other fun activities. In some schools, it's called May Day or Field Day.

Mrs. Walker was very proud of her class. All 24 boys and girls had worked hard all year long and made good grades. However, Mrs. Walker didn't think they worked very well as a team.

Mrs. Walker wanted the day to be fun, but she believed children should learn at every opportunity, even on FUN DAY.

"Aha! That's it," she thought out loud. "Our FUN DAY will be about teamwork—working together to get a job done. Everybody has talents and everybody should learn to work together."

The next day, Mrs. Walker was prepared. "Students, for FUN DAY, we're going to have fun!" Mrs. Walker announced with excitement. All of the students looked at each other with great confusion. After all, FUN DAY was all about having fun.

Then, she said, "I mean real fun! I'm talking about a W-H-O-L-E lot of fun!" as she made a huge gesture in a circle with her arms.

All of the students started pumping their fists in the air, clapping and high-fiving one another, while screaming with excitement.

"Now students, to have fun, we're going to have competitions," Mrs. Walker continued.

"Yeah!" the students yelled. They were getting more excited by the minute.

"Can it be girls against boys, Mrs. Walker?" Carly asked with a big smile on her face.

"No, it won't be girls against boys, Carly," Mrs.Walker replied with a smirk. "I'm going to create four teams with six students on each team.

"We will have a green, blue, red and yellow team," Mrs.Walker further commented. She assigned teams by having them to count-off.

"Now, all of the 'ones' come up front and stand near the blackboard—you are the green team. All of the 'twos' go stand near the globe—you are the blue team. All of the 'threes' go stand near the door—you are the red team. All of the 'fours' go stand near the windows—you are the yellow team," said Mrs. Walker as she pointed toward each location.

"Students, say 'hi' to your teammates. Shake their hands and follow me," Mrs. Walker requested as they all walked down the hallway and out to the playground.

"The first game will be a sack race," explained Mrs. Walker as she pulled out four sacks. "There will be two people per sack and each person must have one leg inside the sack," she directed, lining the students up at the starting line.

"Each pair must go around the pole and come back to the starting line to let the next pair go. The team that completes this race the fastest will be the first place winner and will get 20 points. The team that comes in second will get 15 points, the third place team will get 10 points and the fourth place team will get five points, she explained."

"Ready, set, go!" instructed Mrs. Walker.

The teams started. It took the students a little while to learn to move their legs at the same time as their partners'. Some students tumbled onto the grass. After a while, they learned how to walk together.

Coach Andrews, on his return to the gym, stopped and looked on with amazement.

As the students arrived back at the starting line, they encouraged the other students to do their best. Jermaine, a shy kid on the red team, usually kept to himself. But, during the sack race, he yelled with excitement and offered advice to his team members about how to go faster. With his help, the red team came in first. The blue team came in second. It was a close race between the yellow and green teams.

Finally, the yellow team came in third and the green team came in fourth. The students on the green team started making ugly faces at the students on the yellow team. The students on the yellow team made even uglier faces at the students on the green team.

"That's not good sportsmanship," Mrs. Walker quickly remarked to both teams. She began to wonder whether the competition was a good idea.

As they prepared for the second event, the students on the red team, which came in first place, started celebrating. "Our team is better than your team. We're going to win all of the games," they shouted.

"OK, red team, it's not good to brag," warned Mrs. Walker.

The second event required the teams to spell as many words as they could in five minutes using the letters in the word "dictionary."

"Ready, set, go!" instructed Mrs. Walker.

"I'll write down our words," said Amber to her teammates on the green team.

Jacob, on the yellow team, heard her and decided to do the same for his team. However, his teammate, Carmen, insisted on writing—believing she could write better and faster. The yellow team lost time as Jacob and Carmen argued.

After five minutes, Mrs. Walker ordered all teams to stop. The green team was declared the first place winner, the blue team was second, the red team was third and the yellow team came in fourth.

"Students, this is the last event. It's called 'jellybean in a spoon,'" said Mrs.Walker. "You must keep the jellybean in the plastic spoon while going as fast as you can. You can't keep the jellybean in the spoon from falling with your hand, finger or any other object. If you drop the jellybean, you must pick it up and put it back in the spoon before you can continue. This means you must be very careful.

"When you arrive back at the starting line, pass the spoon and jellybean to your next teammate. And students, please don't eat the jellybeans!" Mrs.Walker added.

"Ready, set, go!" instructed Mrs. Walker.

Allan, on the red team, left the starting line running and dropped his jellybean. He lost his lead after having to go back to pick the candy up. All of the other students quickly realized what would happen if they ran. So, they all started to walk at a very fast pace, some faster than others. All of them were very, very careful.

At the end, the yellow team came in with the big finish. The blue team was second. The green team finished third and the red team finished fourth.

"OK students, let's add the points to see which team is the overall winner," said Mrs. Walker, looking exhausted.

Just then, all of the students realized that they had been so excited about FUN DAY that no one had thought to ask what the prize would be for the winning team.

After the points were added up, the blue team was declared the overall winner.

"Yeah," yelled all of the blue team members as they jumped around with excitement.

Members of the red, green and yellow teams were all disappointed. Nevertheless, as Mrs. Walker gave them a stern look, they clapped for the blue team.

Each member of the blue team received a big bag of jellybeans. Then, the blue team showed kindness by sharing their jellybeans with all of the other students.

"Now students, did you have fun today?" asked Mrs. Walker.

"Yes, ma'am!" responded the children.

"What made this fun for you?" inquired Mrs. Walker.

"I didn't know Jermaine could talk until today," joked Chris. Everybody laughed, including Jermaine.

"Amber helped her team to win by writing real fast," commented Brittany.

"We all did our best to help our team win," shouted Andy with purple jellybeans in his mouth.

Mrs. Walker, now even prouder of her third grade class, smiled as she announced that all of the students were winners and the big prize was a pizza party.

"Let's go to the classroom for pizza!" Mrs. Walker shouted.

Mr. Albert, the principal, stopped by the classroom when he heard music playing. The students were dancing and having a good time.

"Are you having fun, students?" asked Mr. Albert.

"Yes, sir," the excited children replied.

Mr. Albert decided to dance for the students. He started with the *Robot* and finished with the *Running Man*. All the students laughed. They thought he was really funny. After a little while, he left the room holding his back. He had danced a bit too much.

"I'm so proud of all of you," announced Mrs.Walker. "You've learned what teamwork really means. You now know that we all have to work together to win. Yes, this has been a great FUN DAY!

"Yes indeed, this really has been a great FUN DAY!" sighed Mrs.Walker as she relaxed in her chair.